The Adventures of
Brady the
Grasshopper

Written by Maureen Butterfly   Illustrated by Rebecca Miller

HOPPER PRESS
www.bradyhop.com

For Mother and Father - MB

For my husband - RM

Text copyright © 2006 by Maureen J. Olson
Illustrations copyright © 2006 by Rebecca W. Miller

ISBN 0-9790214-0-5

Printed in China

Brady the grasshopper wanted with all his heart
to be a child's pet.
"I'm sorry," said his mother. "Human beings
don't keep grasshoppers as pets."

Brady knew a girl named
Lily, who seemed nice to bugs.

He decided to hop
into Lily's backyard.

"Don't do it!" shouted his father.
"She'll put you in her bug collection!" shouted his mother.

Brady's family members hopped away,
but not Brady!

"Hi Brady!" said Lily.

Lily tried to squeeze Brady into her ant farm,
but he was too big.

He got stuck.

The ants thought he looked like a delicious meal.

Lily popped Brady back out with a barrette.

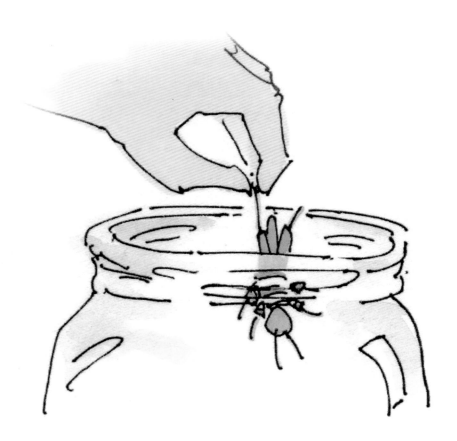

She found a glass jar and dropped Brady inside.

Lily ran into the kitchen to show her family.

"Aaaaa!" screamed her sister, Melody.

"Ba-ba-ba!" said Baby George, which meant, "Can I eat him?"

"No!" cried Lily. "He's my new pet!"

Everything looked funny inside the little glass jar.
Brady shook his head over and over again.
He got so dizzy he fell down.

"Maybe we can build him a bigger home," said Mother.
"No!" Melody protested. "We already have too many bugs!"
"I'll keep him in my room," said Lily.
"The bugs get tired of your room, and they come into my room!"
Melody complained.
"I'll be more careful," Lily promised.

Mother and Lily made Brady a home
out of an old aquarium. They called
it a terrarium.

Lily put in a tiny rolypoly bug named Giganta, a snail
named Alf, a lady bug named Hubie, and a chrysalis.
Then she put Brady inside and put the glass lid on top.

Brady quickly made friends.
He was so happy that he jumped for joy!

Then
something terrible
happened.

Brady smashed into the glass ceiling . . .

. . . and fell into the dirt, unconscious!

"Brady! Brady!"

"What's unconscious?" asked Hubie.
"It means," explained Giganta,
"that he can't hear us or see us,
and he doesn't wake up when we shake him!"
"What should we do?" asked Alf.

Giganta saw a leaf with a drop of water on it. She bit it off
and splashed the drop of water over Brady's face.

Brady woke up.
"What happened?" he asked, rubbing the bump
on his head.
"You hit the glass ceiling," said Alf.
"You shouldn't hop," said Giganta, shaking her finger.

The bugs wanted Brady
to feel better.

Alf tied a piece of grass around
Brady's head as a bandage.

Hubie brought another drop
of water for him to drink.

Giganta sang
him a lullaby.

The next morning when Brady woke up, Giganta said,
"Remember! Don't hop!"
"Okay," Brady mumbled.

Then Lily woke up.
Suddenly, Brady felt so happy he forgot
what he had promised two seconds earlier.
He jumped for joy!

He hit the glass ceiling!

And he fell unconscious to the dirt again!
This time it took three drops of water to wake him up.
A second bump grew bigger and bigger on Brady's head
next to the first one.
He had a terrible headache.

The bugs bandaged him up and dragged him under a leaf to rest.
The chrysalis hung right over his head.
After awhile, it began to quiver.
"What's happening?" Brady asked, frightened.

"I don't know!"
cried Hubie.

"It's an earthquake!"
shouted Alf.

"No it's not!"
Giganta giggled.

The chrysalis quivered
and quivered.

Suddenly, it cracked down the middle. A mysterious black shape pushed its way out!

Hubie and Alf screamed and ran behind a plant to hide.
"It's a monster!" cried Hubie.
"It's an alien from another planet!" cried Alf.
"No it's not!" Giganta giggled.

It was a butterfly!

"Hello, my name is Gloria," said the butterfly
in a sleepy voice.

"Welcome to our terrarium," said Giganta.

"My name is Giganta, and these are
Hubie, Alf and Brady."

"Pleased to meet you all," Gloria said, "but I can't stay long. Lily promised that once I became a butterfly, she would take me back outside."

Suddenly, Brady remembered his life in the vacant lot behind Lily's backyard. He remembered cool breezes and warm sunshine. He remembered his family. He remembered hopping as much as he wanted to, all over the neighborhood.

The next morning, Gloria said, "My wings are dry now."
"Yes," said Brady sadly. "You get to go back outside."
"Maybe you can come, too," Gloria suggested.
"Why don't you climb up on this plant next to me?"

Later that morning, Brady and Gloria waved good-bye to their friends.

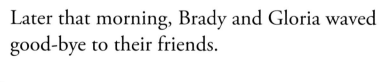

"Don't forget about us!" cried Giganta. "Be sure to write!" cried Alf.

Brady became a legend among
grasshoppers. He told the story of his
two big bumps to all the bugs
in the neighborhood.